基珀的下雪天

米克·英克彭撰文

This edition published in 1996 by
Magi Publications
22 Manchester Street, London W1M 5PG

© Mick Inkpen, 1996
© Chinese translation, Magi Publications, 1996

First published in Great Britain in 1996 by
Hodder Children's Books, London

Manufactured in China

ISBN 1 85430 513 1

Kipper's Snowy Day

Mick Inkpen

Translated by East Word

新的一天來到了。

天上在下著雪!

大片大片棉花羊毛雪花飄過了
基珀的窗口。

"好呀!" 基珀説,跳出了他的小筐。

"好呀! 好呀!" 他抓起了他的圍巾,
在脖子上繞了三圈。 "真、真、 真好!" 基珀
對雪非常喜歡。

It was a new morning and it was snowing!
Huge cotton wool snowflakes were tumbling
past Kipper's window.
"Yes!" said Kipper, jumping out of his basket.
"Yes! Yes!" He grabbed his scarf and wound it
three times round his head. "Yes! Yes! Yes!"
Kipper was very positive about snow.

基珀衝到門外。大雪鋪得很深，

很平坦，很新，就像一張白紙，可以在

上面塗寫。他弄了個腳印，然後又弄一個。

Kipper rushed outside.
The snow lay deep and smooth and new,
like an empty page waiting to be scribbled on.
He made a paw print, and then another.

然後隨著一聲呼叫，他開始衝鋒，

左衝右拐，直到整個花園到處是他的足跡。

And then with a whoop he went charging round and round, crisscrossing this way and that, until the garden was full of his tracks.

基珀停下來喘口氣，讓飄忽
的雪花融化在他的舌頭上。
然後他向後倒在雪裡，大口地喘著氣。
當他站起來後，他發現自己做了一個完整
的基珀雪印。他又做了一個。然後做了一個不
同的形狀。又做了一個。
"我擔保小虎還沒想出這個主意，" 他說，就匆匆
地跑去找他最好的朋友。

Kipper stopped to catch his breath, letting the swirling
snowflakes melt on his tongue. Then he fell backwards
into the snow and lay there panting. When he stood
up he found that he had made a perfect Kipper shaped
hole. He tried again. Then he tried a different shape.
And another.
"I bet Tiger hasn't thought of this," he said, and ran off
to find his best friend.

基珀在小山頂上
找到了小虎。他身上
穿著厚厚的，傻乎乎、
毛絨絨的衣服。基珀好玩地把一個雪球放
在他朋友的頭上。

小虎說："你好!"

小虎指指天空。水淋淋的太陽透過灰灰
的雲在照射。"雪不會下得很久，"他説。"到明天
就全没了。有一股暖風正在吹來。"小虎就是這樣。
他知道這些事情。

Kipper found Tiger at the top of Big Hill. He was
wrapped up in a fat bundle of silly, woolly clothes.
Kipper plopped a friendly snowball on top of his head.
"Hello," said Tiger.
Tiger pointed up at the sky. A watery sun was seeping
through the grey clouds. "It won't last," he said.
"It'll all be gone by tomorrow. There's a warm wind
coming." Tiger was like that. He knew things.

但基珀卻不喜歡聽這種話，於是他開始向他的朋友扔雪球。雪球很容易扔中小虎，因爲那些傻乎乎、毛絨絨的衣服緊緊地裹在他的身上，使他幾乎無法動彈。而他自己的雪球像小絨球一樣黏在傻乎乎、毛絨絨的手套上。

But this was not at all what Kipper wanted to hear, so he started throwing snowballs at his friend. Tiger was very easy to hit because the silly, woolly clothes were wrapped so tightly around him that he could hardly move. And his own snowballs stuck like little pompoms to the silly, woolly gloves.

"看我的新遊戲，" 基珀
説著就往後仰倒在雪裡。
"你得小心地爬起來......
這就成了!" 他，或者説他的模樣
就在雪地裡。
小虎伸展出手臂，象軟棉花似地 "撲騰"
向後倒去。但當他想起來時，卻爬不起來。他太圓
滾滾了。他像翻了個兒的甲蟲一樣，四肢亂舞。

"Look at my new game," said Kipper, falling backwards
into the snow. "You get up very carefully . . . and
there you are!" And there he was, or at least the shape
of him.
Tiger stretched out his arms, and fell backwards with
a soft, woolly 'crump'. But when he tried to get up he
could not. He was too round. He just lay there waving
his arms and legs like a beetle on its back.

小虎費力地翻了個身，但翻過了頭，

又朝天躺著了。他又試了一下，還是這樣。

雪開始厚厚地黏在他的傻乎乎、毛絨絨的

衣服上。他有點生氣了，一用勁又翻了過去。

這一次他翻了兩翻，三翻，四翻……

Tiger heaved himself over onto his tummy, but
rolled too far, and found himself on his back again.
He tried again. The same thing happened. Snow
began to stick in thick lumps to the silly, woolly
clothes. Crossly, he heaved himself over once more.
This time he rolled over twice, three times, four
times . . .

開始很慢，

然後快些，然後更快，

然後很快，一直滾到了山腳下。

在往下滾的時候，那傻乎乎、毛絨絨的衣

服黏到的雪越來越多，當滾到山腳的時候他已經

從一隻小狗變成了一個大雪球。大雪球碎了。

Slowly at first, and then a little faster, and then a
lot faster, and then very fast indeed, he rolled down
the hill. And as he went the silly, woolly clothes
picked up more and more snow, so that by the time
he reached the bottom he had changed from a small
dog into a giant snowball. The giant snowball fell
to pieces.

基珀衝下山去。

"你怎麼樣，小虎?" 他叫道。小虎脫去了他的

傻乎乎、毛絨絨的帽子。他咧嘴笑了。

"再來一次!" 他説。

Kipper charged down the hill.
"Are you all right, Tiger?" he panted. Tiger pulled off
his silly, woolly hat. A big grin spread across his face.
"Again!" he said.

那天，他們就做了這些，輪流穿上那些
傻乎乎、毛絨絨的衣服。
當太陽逐漸碰到山頂，拉長他們的身影時，
他們已經把許多雪滾到山腳，
做了一個大大的雪狗。
他們眼看自己的身影越來越長，最後消失。
小虎說：“到明天就全沒了。有一股暖風正
在吹來。”

So that is what they did, all day long, taking
turns to wear the silly, woolly clothes.
And by the time the sun began to dip towards
the hill, making their shadows long and skinny,
they had rolled enough snow to the bottom to
build a giant snowdog.
They watched their shadows lengthen and fade.
"It'll all be gone by tomorrow," said Tiger.
"There's a warm wind coming."

但這一次小虎錯了。

暖風沒有來，那天晚上又有

一場大風雪，把花園又一次變得像

一張乾淨、白色、無字的紙。

那隻雪狗也呆在大山腳下，身上穿著小虎那傻

乎乎、毛絨絨的衣服......

But for once Tiger was wrong. The warm wind stayed
away, and that night another snowstorm smoothed
out all of Kipper's paw prints, making the garden like
a clean, white, empty page once more.
And the snowdog stood at the bottom of Big Hill
wearing Tiger's silly, woolly clothes . . .

呆了差不多整整......　　　　　三個......

For almost three . . .　　　　　whole . . .

星期。

weeks.